P9-AET-199

Dear Parent:
Your child's love of reading starts here!

Every child learns to read in a different way and at his or her own speed. Some go back and forth between reading levels and read favorite books again and again. Others read through each level in order. You can help your young reader improve and become more confident by encouraging his or her own interests and abilities. From books your child reads with you to the first books he or she reads alone, there are I Can Read Books for every stage of reading:

SHARED READING
Basic language, word repetition, and whimsical illustrations, ideal for sharing with your emergent reader

BEGINNING READING
Short sentences, familiar words, and simple concepts for children eager to read on their own

READING WITH HELP
Engaging stories, longer sentences, and language play for developing readers

READING ALONE
Complex plots, challenging vocabulary, and high-interest topics for the independent reader

ADVANCED READING
Short paragraphs, chapters, and exciting themes for the perfect bridge to chapter books

I Can Read Books have introduced children to the joy of reading since 1957. Featuring award-winning authors and illustrators and a fabulous cast of beloved characters, I Can Read Books set the standard for beginning readers.

A lifetime of discovery begins with the magical words "I Can Read!"

Visit www.icanread.com for information
on enriching your child's reading experience.

Good Driving, Amelia Bedelia

by Herman Parish
pictures by Lynn Sweat

HarperCollins*Publishers*

Watercolors and a black pen were used for the full-color art.

HarperCollins®, 🐾®, and I Can Read Book® are trademarks of HarperCollins Publishers.

Good Driving, Amelia Bedelia Text copyright © 1995 by Herman S. Parish III Illustrations copyright © 1995 by Lynn Sweat All rights reserved. No part of this book may be used or reproduced in any manner whatsoever without written permission except in the case of brief quotations embodied in critical articles and reviews. Manufactured in China. For information address HarperCollins Children's Books, a division of HarperCollins Publishers, 195 Broadway, New York, NY 10007. www.harpercollinschildrens.com

Library of Congress Cataloging-in-Publication Data

Parish, Herman.
  Good driving, Amelia Bedelia / by Herman Parish ; pictures by Lynn Sweat.
    p.   cm.—(An I can read book)
  Summary: Amelia Bedelia's literalness causes some problems when Mr. Rogers takes her out to practice her driving.
  ISBN-10: 0-688-13358-4 (trade bdg.) — ISBN-13: 978-0-688-13358-0 (trade bdg.)
  ISBN-10: 0-06-008092-2 (pbk.) — ISBN-13: 978-0-06-008092-1 (pbk.)
  [1. Automobile driving—Fiction. 2. Humorous stories.] I. Sweat, Lynn, ill. II. Title.
PZ7.P2185 Go 1995   94-4112
[E]—dc20   CIP
                                                                                                                    AC

16 SCP 20

❖

Originally published by Greenwillow Books, an imprint of HarperCollins Publishers, in 1995.

FOR PEGGY PARISH,
THE REAL AMELIA BEDELIA
– H. P.

FOR KEVIN PHILLIP
AND AMANDA LYNN
–L. S.

Good Driving, Amelia Bedelia

Amelia Bedelia

walked into the kitchen.

Mr. and Mrs. Rogers sang out,

"Happy birthday, Amelia Bedelia!"

"Thank you," said Amelia Bedelia.

"Take the day off to celebrate,"

said Mrs. Rogers.

"I'll go and visit my cousin Alcolu," said Amelia Bedelia.

"Use our car," said Mr. Rogers.

"Oh, I have not driven in years," said Amelia Bedelia.

"Is your license still good?"

asked Mrs. Rogers.

"It's great!" said Amelia Bedelia.

"See how nice my picture looks."

"Your license is fine," said Mr. Rogers.
"Let's see if your driving
is as good as your picture.
Meet me at the car.
A short drive in the country
will do you good."

They backed out of the driveway

and away they went.

Amelia Bedelia drove very carefully.

"What a beautiful farm,"

said Mr. Rogers.

"Yes," said Amelia Bedelia.

"And what a nice bunch of cows."

"*Herd* of cows," said Mr. Rogers.

"Heard of cows?"

asked Amelia Bedelia.

"Of course I have heard of cows."

"No," said Mr. Rogers.

"I mean a cow *herd*."

"So what if a cow heard?"

said Amelia Bedelia.

"I didn't say anything bad."

Some cows had wandered onto the road.

"Watch out!" said Mr. Rogers.

Amelia Bedelia stopped the car.

"Steer straight ahead," said Mr. Rogers.

"No," said Amelia Bedelia.

"The steer is behind us."

A cow with big horns
looked into the car.
"Push on the horn," said Mr. Rogers.
Amelia Bedelia gently pushed
on the cow's horn.
MOOOOOOOOOOOOOOO!

Mr. Rogers pushed hard

on the car's horn.

HOOOOOOOOOOOOOOONK!

The cows ran back into the field.

Mr. Rogers took out a road map.

"I am looking for a crossroad,"

he said. "It will have signs

to tell us where to go."

"While you look, I'll go for a walk,"

said Amelia Bedelia.

"Get some directions if you can,"

said Mr. Rogers.

Amelia Bedelia was back

in five minutes. "I did not find

a cross road," she said.

"They were all very nice.

But I got lots of directions.

Would you like

a 'North' or a 'South'?

And I have a nice 'Southeast.'"

"*Now* we are lost," said Mr. Rogers.

"I have no idea where we are!"

"I know where we are,"

said Amelia Bedelia.

"We are right here."

Mr. Rogers looked back at his map.

They got back in the car.

"Should I look for another nice road?"

asked Amelia Bedelia.

"Don't you dare," said Mr. Rogers.

"Look for a fork in the road."

"I once looked for a needle

in a haystack," said Amelia Bedelia.

"I never did find it."

Mr. Rogers pointed straight ahead.

"There is the fork," he said.

Amelia Bedelia looked very hard.

She saw that the road split

into two roads.

"Which road is the fork in?"
asked Amelia Bedelia.

"This road," said Mr. Rogers.

"I don't see any forks *or* spoons,"
said Amelia Bedelia.

"Which way should I turn?"

"Turn left," said Mr. Rogers.

"Left?" asked Amelia Bedelia.

"Right," said Mr. Rogers.

"Okay, I will turn right,"
said Amelia Bedelia.

"Not *right*," said Mr. Rogers.

"Right is *not* right!"

"Well, right is not left,"
said Amelia Bedelia.

"That's right," said Mr. Rogers.

"Left *is* right! Right is *wrong*!"

"I am really mixed up,"
said Amelia Bedelia.

"Right is wrong? Left is right?

Which way should I turn?"

"Bear left!" shouted Mr. Rogers.
So Amelia Bedelia
made a sharp turn . . .
to the right.

"Amelia Bedelia!" shouted Mr. Rogers.

"Why did you turn right?"

"Because," said Amelia Bedelia,

"you warned me about the bear."

"*What* bear?" asked Mr. Rogers.

"You said there was a bear

on the left," said Amelia Bedelia.

"There was no *bear*!"

yelled Mr. Rogers. "I said bear *left*."

"Oh," said Amelia Bedelia.

"If I'd known that the bear had left,

I would not have turned right."

Mr. Rogers was about to blow up.
The tire beat him to it.

KAAAAA-POWIE!

Thump! Thump! Thump!

"A flat tire!" said Mr. Rogers.

He got out to put on the spare.

Mr. Rogers opened the trunk.

He let out a big yell.

"What's wrong?"

asked Amelia Bedelia.

"Did that bear come back?"

"Where is the spare tire?"

asked Mr. Rogers.

"And where is the jack?"

"I don't know where Jack went,"

said Amelia Bedelia.

"Mrs. Rogers took everything

out of the trunk yesterday.

She said she had a lot to buy

at the party store."

Mr. Rogers let out a sigh.

"This has been a long drive
in the country," said Amelia Bedelia.

"The walk back to town
will be even longer," said Mr. Rogers.

"Stay here. I'll go and get help."

"Good luck," said Amelia Bedelia.

Mr. Rogers disappeared down the road.

Minutes later Amelia Bedelia

heard something coming.

It was not Mr. Rogers.

It was not even a car.

It was a tow truck.

"Need any help?" asked the driver.

"That depends," said Amelia Bedelia.

"Are you a Jack?"

"My name is John," he said.

"But you can call me Jack for short."

"I don't care how tall you are,"

said Amelia Bedelia.

"If you are a Jack, you'll do."

Jack looked at the flat tire.

He pulled out a big nail.

"Here is your problem," said Jack.

"A nail?" said Amelia Bedelia.

"I thought I ran over

a fork in the road."

Jack smiled. "Do you have

a spare tire?"

"I'd like to give you one,"

said Amelia Bedelia.

"But we don't have enough good tires

for ourselves."

Jack smiled again. "Would you like me
to give you a tow?"
"I've got all the toes I need,"
said Amelia Bedelia.
"But could you pull our car
back to town?"

"Good idea," said Jack.

He hooked up the car.

They drove down the road

and picked up Mr. Rogers.

Then they headed for home.

There was a big crowd
outside the Rogers house.
"Looks like a party," said Jack.
"How wonderful!"
said Amelia Bedelia.

Mr. Rogers got out of the truck.

"Good heavens!" said Mrs. Rogers.

"You look run down!"

"Don't say that
around Amelia Bedelia,"
said Mr. Rogers. "She might do it."

"Happy birthday, Amelia Bedelia!"
said Cousin Alcolu.

"Hello, Cousin Alcolu,"
said Amelia Bedelia.

"Mr. Rogers was helping me
practice my driving
so I could come to see you.
But we didn't get very far."

"That's okay," said Cousin Alcolu.
"I can drive. I can come to see you
anytime you want.
You will not have to drive at all."

Mr. Rogers shook his hand.

"Thank you, Cousin Alcolu.

It may be Amelia Bedelia's birthday,

but you just gave me the

best present ever."

Amelia Bedelia cut giant slices
of birthday cake for everyone.
And nobody had to go out
to the road to find a fork.

Read all the books about

Amelia Bedelia

Amelia Bedelia
by Peggy Parish
pictures by Fritz Siebel

Thank You, Amelia Bedelia
by Peggy Parish
pictures by Barbara Siebel Thomas

Amelia Bedelia and the Surprise Shower
by Peggy Parish
pictures by Barbara Siebel Thomas

Come Back, Amelia Bedelia
by Peggy Parish
pictures by Wallace Tripp

Play Ball, Amelia Bedelia
by Peggy Parish
pictures by Wallace Tripp

Teach Us, Amelia Bedelia
by Peggy Parish
pictures by Lynn Sweat

Good Work, Amelia Bedelia
by Peggy Parish
pictures by Lynn Sweat

Amelia Bedelia Helps Out
by Peggy Parish
pictures by Lynn Sweat

Amelia Bedelia and the Baby
by Peggy Parish
pictures by Lynn Sweat

Amelia Bedelia Goes Camping
by Peggy Parish
pictures by Lynn Sweat

Merry Christmas, Amelia Bedelia
by Peggy Parish
pictures by Lynn Sweat

Amelia Bedelia's Family Album
by Peggy Parish
pictures by Lynn Sweat

Good Driving, Amelia Bedelia
by Herman Parish
pictures by Lynn Sweat

Bravo, Amelia Bedelia!
by Herman Parish
pictures by Lynn Sweat

Amelia Bedelia 4 Mayor
by Herman Parish
pictures by Lynn Sweat

Calling Doctor Amelia Bedelia
by Herman Parish
pictures by Lynn Sweat

Amelia Bedelia, Bookworm
by Herman Parish
pictures by Lynn Sweat

Happy Haunting, Amelia Bedelia
by Herman Parish
pictures by Lynn Sweat

Amelia Bedelia, Rocket Scientist?
by Herman Parish
pictures by Lynn Sweat

Amelia Bedelia Under Construction
by Herman Parish
pictures by Lynn Sweat

Herman Parish

was in the fourth grade when his aunt, Peggy Parish, wrote the first book about Amelia Bedelia. The lovable, literal-minded housekeeper has been a member of his family ever since. Peggy Parish died in 1988. She would be proud and delighted to know that her nephew is carrying on with Amelia Bedelia in titles including *Bravo, Amelia Bedelia!*; *Amelia Bedelia, Rocket Scientist?*; and *Amelia Bedelia, Bookworm.*

Lynn Sweat

has illustrated many Amelia Bedelia books, including *Bravo, Amelia Bedelia!*; *Amelia Bedelia and the Baby*; and *Amelia Bedelia, Rocket Scientist?* He is a painter as well as an illustrator, and his paintings hang in galleries across the country. He and his wife live in Connecticut.